GINGER
and
PETUNIA

To my friend, Virginia Vincent Folsum, and her pet pig, Petunia.

Patricia Lee Gauch, Editor

PHILOMEL BOOKS
A division of Penguin Young Readers Group. Published by The Penguin Group.
Penguin Group (USA) Inc., 375 Hudson Street, New York, NY 10014, U.S.A.
Penguin Group (Canada), 90 Eglinton Avenue East, Suite 700, Toronto, Ontario, Canada M4P 2Y3 (a division of Pearson Penguin Canada Inc.).
Penguin Books Ltd, 80 Strand, London WC2R 0RL, England.
Penguin Ireland, 25 St. Stephen's Green, Dublin 2, Ireland (a division of Penguin Books Ltd.).
Penguin Group (Australia), 250 Camberwell Road, Camberwell, Victoria 3124, Australia (a division of Pearson Australia Group Pty Ltd).
Penguin Books India Pvt Ltd, 11 Community Centre, Panchsheel Park, New Delhi - 110 017, India.
Penguin Group (NZ), Cnr Airborne and Rosedale Roads, Albany, Auckland 1310, New Zealand (a division of Pearson New Zealand Ltd).
Penguin Books (South Africa) (Pty) Ltd, 24 Sturdee Avenue, Rosebank, Johannesburg 2196, South Africa.
Penguin Books Ltd, Registered Offices: 80 Strand, London WC2R 0RL, England.

Published simultaneously in Canada. Manufactured in China by South China Printing Co. Ltd.
Design by Semadar Megged. Text set in 15.5-point Adobe Jenson. The illustrations are rendered in pencils and markers.

Library of Congress Cataloging-in-Publication Data
Polacco, Patricia. Ginger and Petunia / Patricia Polacco. p. cm. Summary: When her beloved Ginger, a piano-playing socialite and very snappy dresser, makes a last-minute trip to London not knowing her housesitter has cancelled, Petunia the pig does more than fend for herself, she becomes Ginger.
[1. Pigs—Fiction. 2. Human-animal relationships—Fiction. 3. Celebrities—Fiction.
4. Humorous stories.] I. Title. PZ7.P75186Gin 2007 [E]—dc22 2006024878
ISBN 978-0-399-24539-8
3 5 7 9 10 8 6 4 2

Patricia Polacco
GINGER and PETUNIA
Philomel Books

Virginia Vincent Folsum is a very elegant lady!

She lives in a scrumptious home in a very exclusive neighborhood.

Ginger, as she is called, drives a snappy little red sports car, collects fine wines and is a gourmet cook.

But clothes, beautiful clothes are her PASSION!

"You are what you wear," she always says.

She is also a brilliant pianist who gave up the stage to teach a dazzling array of musical prodigies. She accepts only the most promising young musicians. Her waiting list is endless.

She hears her students from 7:30 in the morning until 5:00 in the afternoon.

She listens . . .

and listens . . .

and listens!

But the most astonishing thing about Ginger is Petunia. Her pet pig!

Petunia lives right in Ginger's house, just under the staircase next to the grand piano. Ginger does everything for Petunia. She cooks for her. She sews blankets for her and takes her for rides in her little red car.

Ginger models every new outfit she buys for Petunia first.

And practically every evening they listen to grand opera together.

Ginger even had a mud hole installed in her backyard just for Petunia.

Of course she built a lovely gazebo over the top of it and made it look like a spa.

"My Petunia does so love her mud soaks," Ginger always says.

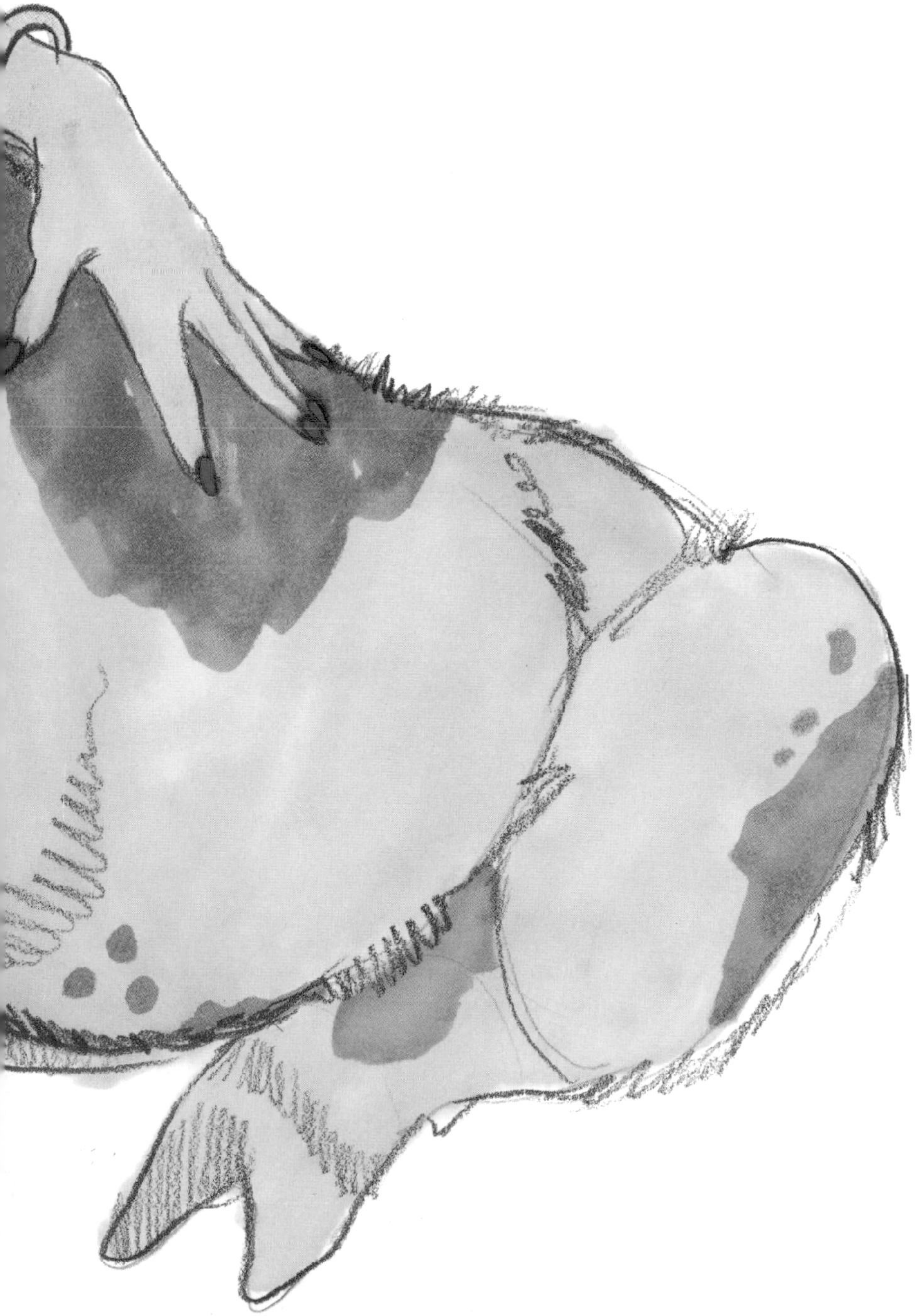

One day, an engraved invitation arrived for Ginger all the way from England.

"I've been invited to be the guest soloist at the International Congress of Pianists . . . in LONDON!" Ginger trumpeted.

Ginger was beside herself with excitement. "But I will have to leave for England tomorrow and, oh dear, there's no food in the house . . . and a whole week of lessons will have to be rescheduled, and there's all of my social obligations . . . and you, Petunia. Who is going to take care of you!" Ginger cried.

In no time, Ginger called Housesitters, Inc. and arranged for someone to come and take care of Petunia and do everything on her to-do list.

The next morning, it was time for Ginger to catch her flight. "Well, my dear Petunia . . . I will miss you so very much," Ginger whispered as she kissed her pig's snout. "Someone will be here within the hour to take care of you. I'll be back before you know it."

Petunia watched as the cab left for the airport. The house was so empty. It was so quiet. This was the very first time Ginger had ever gone away and left Petunia. She went to her little room under the stairs, cuddled under her favorite blanket and waited for the housesitter to arrive. She waited and waited and waited.

But no one came.

Just then the phone rang, and a raspy voice left a message.

"Mrs. Folsum, this is the agency, and . . . well . . . it seems our housesitter will not be able to come. She wasn't very happy about the pig. I'm sure you'll find someone else before you leave." Then she hung up.

Petunia's eyes widened. She curled up in her blanket and thought and thought.

After Petunia had thought for the longest time, she went to the kitchen. She peered into the refrigerator. It was practically empty, just as Ginger had said, but there were a few vegetables in the crisper, three eggs, some flour, a half a quart of milk and a bottle of rare wine.

A wry smile crept across Petunia's face as she put on Ginger's apron. Petunia chopped vegetables as she had seen Ginger do so many times. Then she sautéed them in virgin olive oil just the way Ginger had shown her. She made pasta from scratch and made perfect angel hair spaghetti—just as Ginger did. She made a salad of baby greens, walnuts and dried cherries, and poured herself a glass of that rare wine.

Then she set herself a place at the counter, lit the candles and sipped her chardonnay. "An impudent little wine . . . insistent, yet witty . . . with just a hint of grass, yet buttery," Petunia mused to herself. Then she put on her favorite opera and ate her pasta. When she finished dinner, she got up and erased the phone message from the agency.

The next morning Petunia went into Ginger's closet. She put on one of Ginger's elegant outfits. Getting Ginger's makeup just right was the hardest part. She donned one of Ginger's stunning silk scarves. Then the doorbell rang and Petunia saw through the peephole that it was Ginger's first student of the day. Petunia let him in.

He went straight to the piano, opened the music and commenced to play. Petunia listened and nodded at precisely the right times. She pointed out the notes that he missed. When the lesson was over, Petunia pointed at the clock and the lad left.

And so it went all day long. Petunia listened to each of Ginger's students.

Conceal Powder
Hair Remover
Eye Cream

She listened . . .

and listened . . .

and listened.

By the time Petunia heard the last student of the day, she was craving a soak in her glorious mud! But just as she was getting ready to peel off Ginger's clothes and leap into her beloved, bubbling muck, she remembered that there was no food in the house!

So Petunia put on one of Ginger's loveliest hats and favorite sunglasses and found the perfect handbag. She grabbed the car keys from the hall table, leapt into the little red car and off she went to the grocery store.

At the store, Petunia picked only the freshest and firmest fruits and vegetables, just as she had seen Ginger do. She got everything on Ginger's list. The grocery clerk was cheery and referred to her as Mrs. Folsum and even helped her out with the bags of groceries.

Petunia smiled, tossed him a very generous tip, climbed into the little red car and drove off.

As Petunia opened the door, she heard Ginger leaving a message on the phone—all the way from England.

"Hellooooo," she cooed. "You are probably running some of the errands on my list. I do hope you are taking very good care of dear Petunia. Give her an extra treat from me. Here's my number if you need me: 553-259-3323-69. Chesterton upon Punsey . . ."

Petunia looked at the clock. It was much too late for a mud soak, so after supper she settled in to study Ginger's to-do list. "Call the art museum and explain why I cannot attend the installation ceremony for the new statue on Thursday," it said. That was tomorrow!

Too late to cancel.

So all the next day, Petunia taught lessons, even though she couldn't seem to get her mind off of her beloved mud hole under the gazebo just outside the window.

When the last student left, Petunia tugged off her dress and was finally getting ready to leap into that beloved muck when the doorbell rang. She looked through the peephole. It was the car to pick Ginger up to go to the *museum!*

Petunia threw on a lovely gown, hat and scarf and leapt into the car.

When she arrived, the ceremony was under way. The speeches were endless, and it was hot and stuffy, and so many people! Petunia began to find it hard to stand on her two feet. She'd be so much more comfortable on all fours!

Just as the curator was about to conclude his speech, Petunia teetered.

She was shaky and very, very dizzy. She braced herself against the statue but it wobbled, then toppled to the floor. It shattered into a thousand pieces.

There was a gasp, then total silence as the crowd glared at Petunia.

"Wait," said the docent. "Ancient Roman statues are always made of marble. This is just cheap plaster!"

"A forgery!" someone howled.

"Ginger Folsum," the curator announced, "has saved the day!"

By the time Petunia got home, it was once again too late to soak in her mud spa.

By the next morning, the headlines of the papers read "Virginia Folsum Exposes Forgery!" The phone wouldn't stop ringing. Reporters wanted interviews.

There were endorsement offers from soda companies, paint stores and an athletic shoe company! At noon, an invitation came from the mayor himself for dinner in Ginger's honor. That very evening. A car would pick her up at six o'clock.

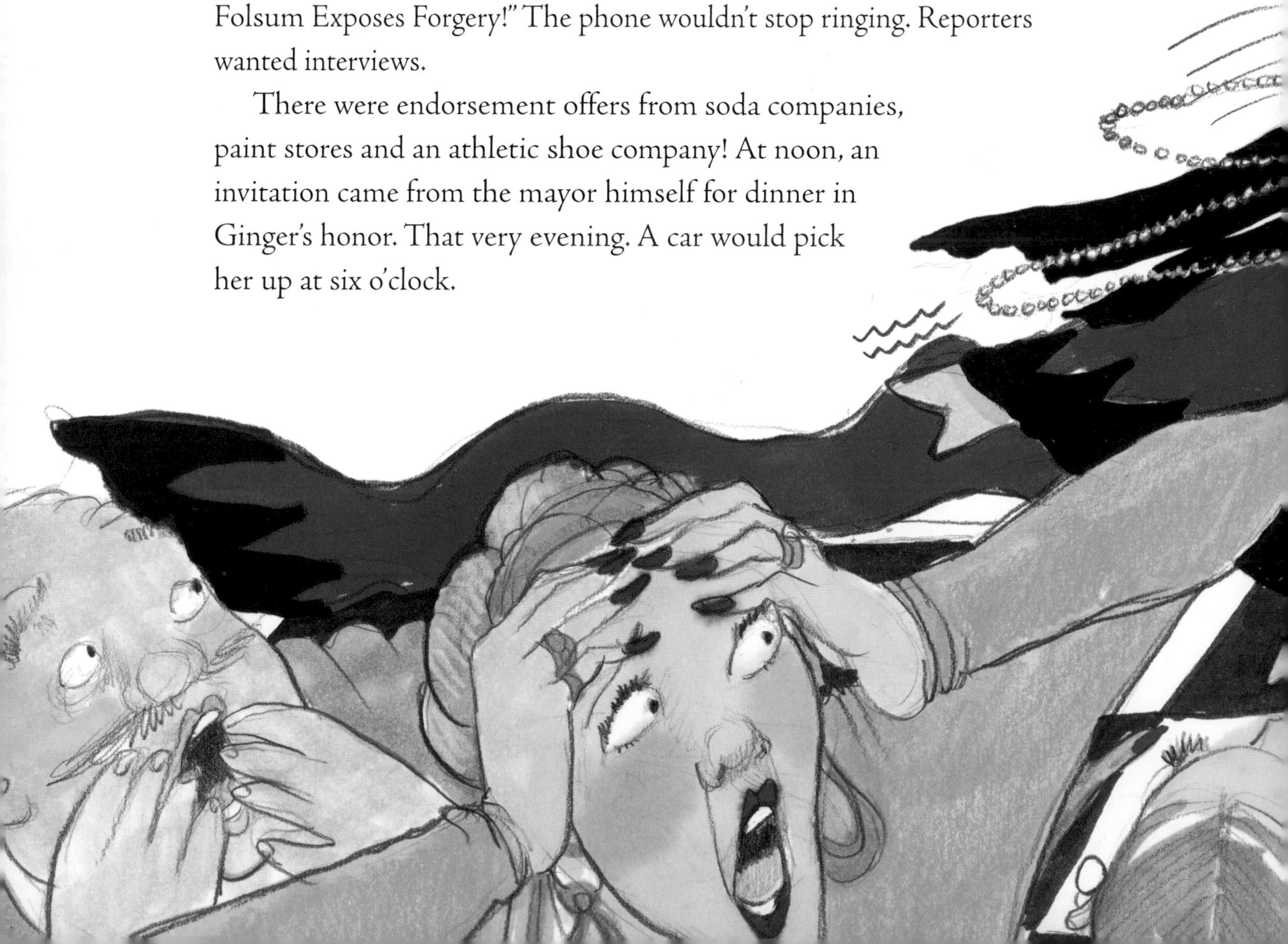

COMMERCE

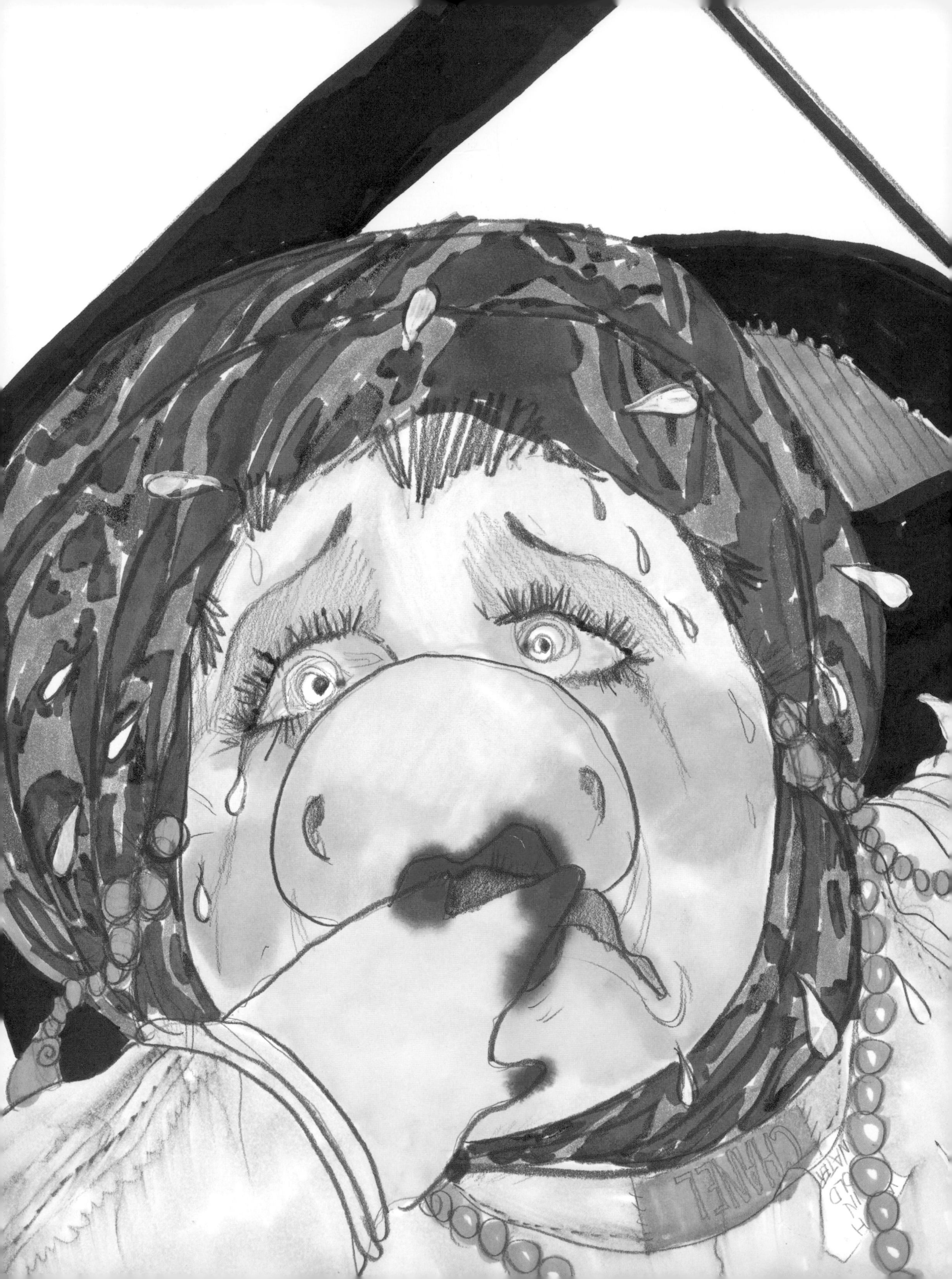
CHANEL

All that day, Petunia was distressed. Mud deprivation does terrible things to a pig. Petunia had put on her dress backwards and nothing matched. When her students arrived, she just stared out the window at her beloved mud hole. She started to grunt, quietly at first, then small squeals. She missed all of the student's wrong notes, and had them play their music upside down.

Finally, the last student left. Petunia was desperate to rip off her clothes and dive into her bubbling, warm, wet, squishy mud. But the doorbell rang. It was the car for the mayor's dinner! Petunia squealed as she dressed. Her snout twitched and she grunted almost uncontrollably.

But she had to go. After all that Ginger had done for her, she couldn't let her down now.

The dinner party was a gala affair. Absolutely everyone wanted to know THE Virginia Folsum. Petunia stood right next to the mayor in the reception line. Except for some small grunting sounds, she was holding it together pretty well. Ginger Folsum—alias Petunia Pig—was, again, a hit.

That is, until they all sat down for dinner. Instead of using her silverware, Petunia suddenly slurped down her soup right from the bowl. Then she gobbled down the main course with loud smacking sounds.

Finally she sat back and let out a huge burp!

At first there was only stunned silence. But then the hostess said, "Mrs. Folsum has just returned from an exotic country. She is merely demonstrating rare foreign customs." Petunia nodded yes. And so, one by one the guests joined Petunia. They slurped their soup right from their bowls, gulped down their food, and one by one they sat back and burped.

"What an original idea to break the ice," one lady sighed.

"Madame," the governor said as he kissed Petunia's hoof. "I want you to be my most esteemed guest at the Black and White Ball tomorrow night. I'll send a car for you at seven."

Of course Petunia got home too late to soak in her mud once again. She spent a very restless night.

The next morning as Petunia heard her students, her nose twitched, her skin itched and she grunted, groaned and squealed. But she listened to every last one of them all day. By the time the car arrived to take her to the governor's Black and White Ball, she looked very glamorous. She had put on one of Ginger's best gowns.

The ball was in full swing when Petunia arrived. She was every inch the lady that she knew Ginger would want her to be . . . until the hors d'oeuvres tray came by. Petunia tipped the entire tray into her gaping mouth. She smacked her lips and made loud grunting sounds. Just as she was about to head for the banquet table, the governor himself came up to her.

"Madame Folsum, the tango is playing. I have heard that this is your favorite dance. Could I have the honor?" he asked with a sweeping bow.

As the tango played, the governor swept Petunia onto the dance floor. The two tangoed from one side of the ballroom to the other in perfect unison. Petunia, haughty and indifferent. The governor, oily and smooth. Their dance was sultry and flawless . . . until Petunia spotted a huge fountain full of chocolate mousse in the center of the banquet hall.

It looked just like mud!

She pulled the governor toward the fountain of deep brown pudding. He dragged her back into the center of the dance floor.

"My dear," he whispered.

Petunia picked him up and twirled him over her head, then tried to run to the chocolate goo. He landed right beside her, tipped her over backwards and dragged her about the floor.

Petunia dragged the governor by his collar back to the chocolate fountain. "You are an exciting dancer, Mrs. Folsum," the governor wheezed.

Petunia grabbed his ankles and swung him round and round and up into the huge vat of chocolate mousse.

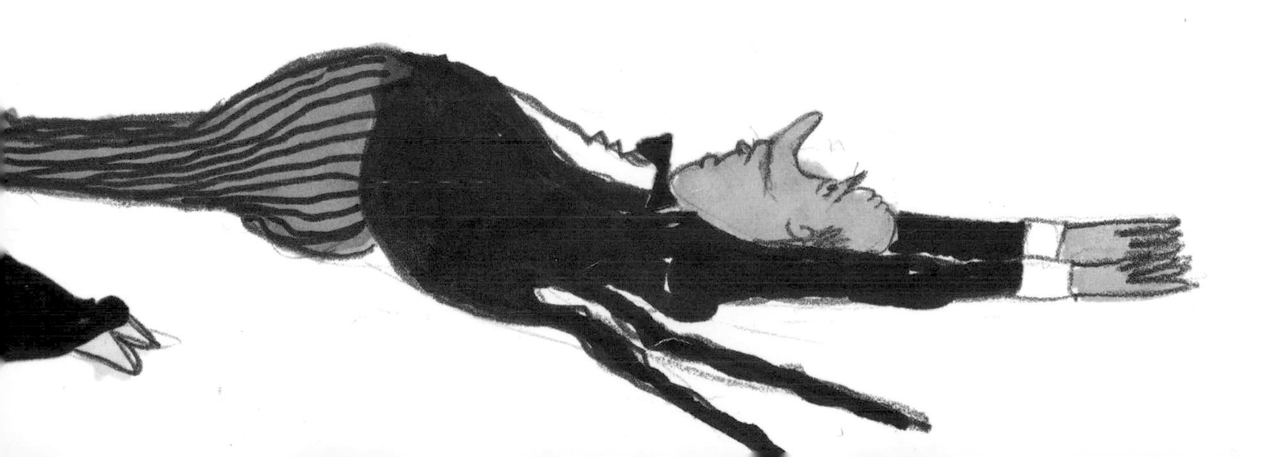

Then Petunia grunted and squealed and dove in after him.
"Now that is a tango!" the governor trumpeted.

Ginger Folsum was yet again the hit of a party. Everyone that was anyone at the ball jumped into the chocolate mousse too!

Petunia should have been a very happy pig, but when she was driving home from the ball, she began to cry. The dishes waited for her, vacuuming waited for her, the whole house waited for her, and she needed a REAL MUD BATH!

But when Petunia stepped into the house, the soft lights were on and opera was playing. The house was clean. The table was set and flowers arranged. A delicious aroma was coming from the kitchen.

Then she heard a very familiar voice. "Petunia, my dear pig. I see you have had quite a time."

It was Ginger! Petunia jumped into her arms.

"You know, my dear, we do get the news in London. I know everything!"

Then Ginger hugged Petunia. "You did exactly what you HAD to do, and I promise that I'll never leave you again."

Petunia nuzzled Ginger and grunted.

"And to think no one noticed that YOU weren't ME! Well, I always say you are what you wear. And, Petunia . . . from what I gather . . . you were a great ME!"

At that very moment, Ginger put on Petunia's favorite opera, and they both had a glorious, long, lovely wallow in the mud . . . together!